Greta Gorsuch

THE CELL PHONE LOT

Greta Gorsuch has taught ESL/EFL and applied linguistics for more than thirty years in Japan, Vietnam, and the United States. Greta's work has appeared in journals such as *System*, *Reading in a Foreign Language*, *Language Teaching*, *Language Teaching Research*, and *TESL-EJ*. She recently co-authored *Second Language Course Evaluation* and *Second Language Testing for Student Evaluation and Classroom Research*. She lives in beautiful wide West Texas and goes camping whenever she can.

First published by GemmaMedia in 2018.

GemmaMedia
230 Commercial Street
Boston MA 02109 USA

www.gemmamedia.com

Printed in the United States of America
978-1-936846-69-6

Library of Congress Cataloging-in-Publication Data

Names: Gorsuch, Greta, author.
Title: The cell phone lot / Greta Gorsuch.
Description: Boston MA : GemmaMedia, 2018. | Series: Gemma Open Door |
   Identifiers: LCCN 2018034030 (print) | LCCN 2018035451 (ebook) | ISBN
   9781936846702 (ebook) | ISBN 9781936846696
Classification: LCC PS3607.O77 (ebook) | LCC PS3607.O77 C45 2018 (print) |
   DDC 813/.6--dc23
LC record available at https://lccn.loc.gov/2018034030

Cover by Laura Shaw Design

Gemma's Open Doors provide fresh stories, new ideas, and essential resources for young people and adults as they embrace the power of reading and the written word.

Brian Bouldrey
Series Editor

GEMMA

Open Door

CHAPTER ONE

Jessica's life was over, and it was only ten in the morning. She sat there in her new red car. The car she saved months for. The car she borrowed money for. The red car with two doors and black seats. The red car with the endless speed. Her little Nissan 370Z.

Jessica didn't start the car. She just sat and looked straight ahead. She could see the back of the Wintergreen Drug Store. There wasn't much to see. The manager at Wintergreen made employees park in the back. Next to the dumpster.

The back of the Wintergreen Drug Store looked different from the front. At the entrance, the windows were large. You wanted to go inside. You could see so many bright things to buy. Candy, cosmetics, shampoo, T-shirts, and cards. In the back of the store, there was just the dumpster. And on this cold February day, the view looked dark and sad. The plain, windowless door was shut tight.

So Jessica sat, thinking that her life was over. She couldn't believe it. What happened? Things *were* going so well. She had a job as the head of the beauty department at five Wintergreen stores. She worked hard to get the job. She went to cosmetology school. She spent a year studying skin care, makeup techniques, and business management. She graduated at the top of her class.

She interviewed at every department store and beauty salon in town. Her older brother, Brandon, said, "See, you messed up again. Why didn't you go to college? No one's going to pay you to do makeup." But then she got a phone call from the manager of cosmetics for Wintergreen Drug Stores. It was a national chain! He invited Jessica to come to the headquarters for an interview.

Her father, Juan Vasquez, drove her the six hours to Dallas in his huge car. Jessica wanted to drive by herself. Since her mother had died two years earlier, her father had become very quiet. Still, he wanted to drive her to Dallas. He said so. And Jessica decided she wanted to spend time with him. It was a silent drive.

They got to Dallas. Jessica had her interview. And she got the job! She was the new beauty and cosmetics manager for Wintergreen Drug Stores in her hometown. When she told her father on the way home, he smiled.

"That's great, Jessica, *amor*," said Juan Vasquez.

Her brother and sister wouldn't believe it when she told them about the job. Jessica was the middle child. She was the one who always messed up. She was the one who hadn't gone to college. She was the one who smoked. Her mother, Victoria Vasquez, yelled at her at least once a week. "You should be in college! Become a lawyer!

Become someone! Stop partying and start studying!" But Jessica spent her last two years of high school going to parties. She didn't study. She found she enjoyed doing her friends' hair. She tried new makeup techniques on them. Her mother just shook her head. Jessica would not be going to college.

When Jessica and her dad got home from Dallas, she called her younger sister, Veronica.

"I don't believe it," said Veronica.

CHAPTER TWO

Jessica loved her job. For over a year, she worked at all five stores. She read about new makeup lines. She ordered makeup and bath products from the main office in Dallas. She decided how to display them in each store. She did makeovers for customers. One lady bought over a hundred dollars' worth of cosmetics after a makeover. Jessica answered questions and made suggestions. She felt great about herself.

Each store was different. One store, in the historic part of town, had mostly older customers. The men mainly wanted shampoo, while the women wanted makeup. Another store, near the college, had mostly young female customers. They wanted makeup and perfume.

Jessica made good money. Brandon, who was a lawyer, made a lot more. Veronica, who was still in college, studied engineering. She told Jessica, "I have a summer job at an engineering company. I'll make more than you." Jessica smiled. Veronica just wanted to believe that. Jessica saw her father once or twice a week. Over dinner, Juan Vasquez listened to Jessica's stories about work. He said, "That's great, Jessica. You seem happy." Then he got quiet again. Jessica washed the dishes. Then she kissed her father before she went home.

She had an apartment at the newest building in town. She didn't know anyone yet. Her neighbors were all young professionals. They were always in a hurry, carrying lattes. Or texting on their expensive smartphones.

So, with all this new brightness in her life, what went wrong?

It all started with the manager's daughter at one of the stores. Against Wintergreen Drug Store rules, the manager hired his own daughter as an employee. The girl went to college but couldn't find a job after she graduated. Her name was Cammie.

Cammie had blond hair and pink lips. Her eyes were blue and hard. She always looked angry. She sometimes had bad skin. Jessica once suggested some skin-care ideas, but Cammie said, "I know more than you!" Then she turned and walked away. Whenever Jessica visited that store, she found Cammie in the makeup section. Cammie picked things up and put them back down. Once or twice, Jessica saw Cammie put something in her pocket. Cammie saw her looking and said, "What are you looking at?"

Jessica said nothing.

"I have a question for you, since you know so much!" said Cammie. "Why do you have this makeup so far away from the door?" She pointed at a new line of makeup from London.

"I don't know why it's there," said Jessica. "That's not where I put it last week."

"Huh!" said Cammie. Then she walked away. Again.

Jessica spent an hour putting the

display back in the right place. Then she wrote what happened in her notebook.

Next, Cammie told her father that Jessica smoked. That she smelled bad. "Who would buy beauty products from her?" she said. Jessica never smoked at work. She shampooed her hair every day. She didn't know how Cammie knew she smoked. Was Cammie going through her purse in the back room?

Then, this morning, the manager walked up to Jessica and said, "Come with me." Jessica stopped working and followed him to the back office.

"Explain this," he said. He pointed at her bag. It was full of makeup and perfume from the store! How did it get there? Jessica didn't know.

"I didn't put that there!" she said.

"Please leave," the manager said. "I'm calling Dallas."

And now Jessica's life was over.

CHAPTER THREE

Sitting in her new red car, Jessica felt sick. She wanted to see her dad. She wanted to tell someone what happened, ask someone what to do. She didn't take anything from the store! She was pretty sure Cammie put the things in her bag and then told the manager that Jessica took them. She had her notes about Cammie. She would call the main office in Dallas! She would tell them what happened.

Jessica drove home. She walked to her apartment. She didn't see any of her neighbors. They were all at work. Jessica called the main office in Dallas. She asked for the extension for Mr. Stamps, the man who hired her.

He came on the line. "Jessica, a

manager just called us. He said you took makeup and perfume from a store. Is that true?"

Jessica did her best to explain. She had her notes. But at the end, she started to cry.

"Ms. Vasquez," said Mr. Stamps, "this is a serious matter. I'll make some phone calls. But I have to tell you, it doesn't look good. Wintergreen Drug Store has rules. Even if I can hire you back, it will take a month or more. I think you need to look for another job."

Jessica hung up. She sat down and cried. It was all so wrong!

After a few hours, she started making phone calls, trying to find another job. She got an interview at a department store the next morning. The manager asked why she left Wintergreen Drug Stores.

"What we pay is only half of what you got at Wintergreen," he said. "This job is sales only. Are you sure you want this job?" Jessica told him yes. But the next day, when she called to find out if she got the job, the man told her, "We called the manager at Wintergreen and he said you stole from the store. We can't have employees who do that." And he hung up.

Two weeks went by. Jessica had two more interviews. But she didn't get either job. Both times, someone called Wintergreen. No one believed Jessica.

Jessica began to run out of money. She had payments to make on her new red car. And her one-room apartment was expensive. She quit smoking because she didn't have the money for it. Life was very hard! To save gas money, she began to walk everywhere. At least that helped her to stop smoking.

During one of her walks to the grocery store, she decided to stop at a small park. As she sat in the sunshine, she saw a car drive by. It had a sign on the windshield that said, "Ryde Driving Service." It was just a medium-sized gray car. A lady was driving it, and someone was sitting in the back. Jessica watched as the car pulled up next to a house. The man in back got out. The driver got out, too. She opened the car's trunk and took out a large suitcase. The man took it and handed the driver some money. Then she drove away.

A driving service! Jessica thought. *Of course! I can work for them driving my own car!*

She found the Ryde Driving Service's website and signed up to be a driver. Within an hour, someone from Ryde called her. "We got your application," said the young man. "And we need another driver in your area. But you're driving a very small car, with only two doors. Usually, people who pay for a ride want a larger car, where they can sit in back."

"Oh," said Jessica. She thought for a minute. "So, if I have a larger car, I can drive for you?"

"Yes, I think so," said the Ryde employee. "You can start tomorrow if you want."

CHAPTER FOUR

That night, Jessica had dinner with her dad. Juan Vasquez was a good cook. Even before his wife died, he did a lot of the cooking. Tonight he made salad, soft rice with tomatoes, and delicious chicken tamales. The tamales were tender and spicy. Jessica and her father agreed that tamales were the perfect food for breakfast, lunch, or dinner. Juan's mother and grandmother in Mexico taught him the recipe. When he came to the United States, he kept on making the tamales. Sometimes he even sold them for money. It was hard to find such perfect tamales, and people paid good money for them.

But Juan's main job was painting houses. When he first came to the

United States, he spoke little English. But he quickly found work painting people's homes. After a few years, he started his own business. Five men worked for him now. He painted over a hundred houses a year. People liked his work. He was good with money. He sent his oldest son to law school. And his youngest daughter was in college. But when Jessica went to cosmetology school, she said she didn't want him to pay for it. She said she could do it herself. And she did.

Just before his wife, Victoria, died, Juan bought a new car. He went to ten different car dealers looking for just the right one. Finally, he found it. It was a silver four-door Genesis. A very large car with soft, wide seats. It was so quiet inside. There was cruise control and a camera for backing up. There were seat heaters and a beautiful radio and CD player. The car was amazing! Juan bought it. He paid cash.

He brought it home to Victoria. She was completely surprised. And she loved the car! She loved driving it. She loved how large and quiet it was. But only a week later, she had a heart attack at work. One minute she was talking, and the next she was gone. Her coworkers called 911. But it was too late.

So now, Juan Vasquez had a large, beautiful car that he hardly ever used. It reminded him too much of Victoria. He was still so sad that she was gone. As he looked at Jessica, he felt sad about her, too. She was so quiet tonight.

She looked thinner. She wasn't wearing any makeup. That surprised Juan Vasquez. Usually Jessica came straight from work. She had nice makeup, a nice hairdo, and nice clothes. Now, she just looked tired.

After dinner was over, Juan asked Jessica, "*Amor*, what's wrong? What's going on?"

Jessica told him everything. She told him about Cammie. She told him about Cammie's father and his phone call to the Wintergreen office in Dallas. She told him she was running out of money.

"When did this all happen?" he asked.

"Three weeks ago," said Jessica.

She told him about her plan to

work for Ryde Driving Service. "But I need a larger car," she said. "They said my Nissan was too small to take passengers."

Juan Vasquez nodded his head. "We will trade cars," he said. "Just for a few weeks. You take the silver Genesis. I will drive your little red car."

Jessica sat in silence. That was what she wanted. But she was surprised that her father had the same idea.

"One other thing," said Juan Vasquez. "You and I are going to the police. You're going to tell them what happened at Wintergreen. I think it's strange that the manager never called the police about you. What's he hiding?"

CHAPTER FIVE

Jessica and her father went to the police together. They spoke with Officer White. They talked about Wintergreen, Cammie, and the manager. Jessica showed him her notes. Officer White was a young man, in his twenties. He listened carefully. Juan Vasquez said that Jessica left Wintergreen three weeks ago.

"Why hasn't the manager called you?" Juan asked Officer White. "If he thought my daughter stole things, why didn't he call the police?"

"Yes, that is a little strange," said Officer White. He had a deep voice. "I'll start a report. And I'll make some phone calls." He looked at Jessica. "You didn't take anything, right?"

"No!" said Jessica, hurt. "I work for everything I have."

"It's true," said Juan Vasquez. "She put herself through cosmetology school. She works very hard."

Officer White looked at Jessica. He had deep blue eyes. Jessica turned a little pink. "I'll call you when I know something," he said after a minute.

Jessica took her father back to his house. She gave him the keys to her fast little red Nissan 370Z. And she drove away in his huge silver Genesis. It was like driving a boat. But she liked it. When she got home, she spent an hour on the computer. When she was done, she was officially a driver for Ryde Driving Service! She sent the company her photograph. She also sent a photograph of the car. She spent another hour cleaning the Genesis. It was already beautiful, but she cleaned it anyway. She took everything out of the inside. She swept all the seats and the floor. She put a small box of tissues in the back. She cleaned the outside of the car. Its silver paint flashed in the sunlight. She washed the windows. Finally, Jessica put a small cooler on the floor in the front of the car. She filled the cooler with ice and bottles of water. *For my passengers*, she thought. The Ryde Driving Service website said she could offer her passengers bottled water.

Then she turned on her Ryde app. Now Ryde Driving Service knew she was ready to accept calls for rides.

Anyone could ask for a ride using the app. They could see a little map with cars. When they clicked on a car, the driver's picture, name, and car information came up. If a passenger wanted to ride with that driver, they clicked a button. Then the driver got a message about where to go. The driver pressed a button to accept the job. Then the passenger knew a driver was coming.

Jessica's first passenger was at the hospital near her apartment. The passenger was an older lady coming home after a treatment. Jessica helped her into the back seat. They stopped at a drug store (not Wintergreen!) for some medicine. Jessica gave the lady a bottle of water. The lady took a few pills and used the water to wash them down. Then Jessica took her to a small house. She helped the lady into her home.

"Thank you," the lady said before closing the door.

"Thanks ma'am, bye," said Jessica.

Jessica checked her Ryde app. She was already paid for the ride! She did her first Ryde drive.

CHAPTER SIX

The next few days were much the same. Jessica cleaned the big silver Genesis. Then she turned on her Ryde app. After a few minutes, she got a message saying she had a passenger. She got five or six passengers each day. She didn't know any of them. One was a younger woman with two small children. She needed a ride to the supermarket. Another was a man who was late to class at the university. "I got up too late," he said to Jessica as she dropped him off at the school's main gate. One passenger was an older man who needed a ride to a car-repair shop. His own car was being fixed. Jessica was paid for each ride through the app.

She gave the older man a second ride later on the same day. He waited for hours at the shop. But his car was still not repaired. "That shop is no good," he said. "Do you know about any other car-repair shops? Anyone who does good work?"

Jessica thought of her father's friend Pablo Cuevas. He was good with cars. He had a small shop. "I know one person," said Jessica. She gave the man Mr. Cuevas' address and phone number. "He's on the east side of town," said Jessica. "I heard he does good work."

"Are you from the east side of town?" asked the man.

"Yes, but I don't live there now," said Jessica. "My father still does." She got her passenger to his house. It was on the west side of town. This was the "rich" side of town. The man's house was large and expensive looking. The yard was full of big, beautiful trees. As he got out of the car, he handed Jessica twenty dollars!

Jessica was stunned. "Thank you," she said.

"You're welcome," said the man, and he went into his house.

A few hours later, Jessica saw five stars by her name! "Helpful and doesn't talk too much," the older man wrote. The older lady at the hospital gave her four stars. Her comment was: "Gave me some cold water and helped me to my door. Nice young woman."

But she needed to make more money. Just that morning she got a note in her mailbox: *Rent is two weeks late. Pay now or leave by the end of the month.* She went to the apartment manager. She paid half of the rent and promised the rest at the end of the week. The apartment manager was a middle-aged woman named Lucy Pettit. She always looked worried, like she had no time for anything. Today she looked angry.

"We can't keep doing this," she told Jessica. "It looks bad. You need to pay your rent, in full."

"I know, ma'am," said Jessica. Her face was red. She wanted to cry. She worked so hard to get this apartment. Now she was in a tough spot.

Lucy was quiet for a minute. Then she said, "You can do makeup, can't you? I saw you at Wintergreen once."

"Yes, ma'am," said Jessica. She was trying to sit up and look okay. Not sad. But she felt sad.

"Well," said Lucy, "my younger sister is getting married next week. And she needs someone to do her makeup. The lady who was supposed to do it left town, so now she has no one. And her four bridesmaids need their makeup done, too. She can pay four hundred dollars, cash. Are you interested?"

Jessica was so surprised that she couldn't speak. Then she said, "Of course! Yes. I'd love to."

"Good," said Lucy. "Here is her

phone number. Please call her as soon as possible. The wedding is coming up, and she's got a lot to do." She handed Jessica a piece of paper. For the first time that day, Lucy smiled.

CHAPTER SEVEN

The job at the wedding would help, but Jessica still needed to make more money. After her talk with Lucy, she turned on her Ryde Driving Service app. She didn't want to drive at night, but she needed the money. She gave three rides, all after ten p.m. The passengers were all university students. They were loud and drunk. They used Ryde Driving Service to go to bars. It was safer than driving home in their own cars. One girl lit a cigarette. Jessica asked her not to smoke in the car. "Oh, okay," said the girl. Jessica wanted to smoke more than anything. It was so tough to quit! But she didn't have the money. And perhaps it was time to quit anyway.

Jessica wanted to go home after the first group of students. They laughed at everything. They were loud. They had stupid conversations. But as soon as she dropped off one group, she got another request on the Ryde app. She was the only Ryde driver in the area. So she went. The second passengers were a young man and his girlfriend. They were drunk. They were having a fight. "Yes, you did! I know you texted her!" said the girl, a blonde who looked a little like Cammie. Jessica sighed. She got them to their college apartment building. They got out of the car without saying "Thank you" or even "Goodbye."

The last passengers were three young men. One of them was the student who Jessica took to school because he was late to class. "Hey!" he said. He was drunk. "I know you! How ya doin'?"

I think I know why you can't get up early enough for classes, thought Jessica.

"Hey!" said the young man. "Guys! I know her!" The other two boys laughed. They were drunk, too. "You're realllllllyyyy cute," said the first. Then he got sick all over the back of the big silver Genesis.

When Jessica got home, she spent an hour cleaning the car. She cleaned and cleaned. Finally, everything came out. Even the smell. *Never again*, she thought. *I'm not working down at the bars again.* She found the passenger on her Ryde app and gave him one star. She wrote in the comments: "Got sick all over my car."

The next morning, she got a call from Ryde. "I'm so sorry," said the Ryde person. "We can pay for any cleaning you need to do," she said.

Jessica sighed. Then she said, "Thank you. I'll need about ten dollars for the cleaning. But I need to make more money. And I don't want to drive drunk passengers. Do you have any suggestions?"

"We see a lot of calls from the airport in your town," said the Ryde person. "Have you tried out there? I think the passengers are mostly business people."

"Thank you!" said Jessica. "I'll try that."

She hung up. Then she got on the airport's website. The airport was completely new to her. But she sort of knew where it was. She found out there were flights every day from Houston, Dallas, Austin, and Oklahoma City. Two flights landed at eight a.m., and three more landed at seven p.m.

She saw a note on the airport's website: "All driving service drivers should wait in the cell phone lot. Do not wait in front of the airport!" A map showed where the cell phone lot was. Jessica decided she would be at the cell phone lot the next morning.

CHAPTER EIGHT

The next morning, Jessica got to the airport at seven a.m. It was still completely dark. She was an hour early for the eight a.m. flights from Dallas and Houston. The airport was fifteen minutes north of town. It was a lonely spot. There weren't any trees, and there were very few houses. The airport was an older building. It was brown and square. Other than that, there was just open country.

Jessica found the cell phone lot. This was a parking lot where people waited until someone they knew arrived on a plane. When their friends or family members landed, they called the person in the cell phone lot. Then the driver went to the front of the airport to pick them up.

To Jessica's surprise, the cell phone lot was very nice. It was just a parking lot, of course. But there were trees all around it. And there was a clean bathroom and a picnic table! It was a small, green park in the middle of nowhere.

Jessica was also surprised to find three people already sitting at the picnic table. They were all drivers for Ryde Driving Service. There was an older man, a young man, and a middle-aged woman. They were sharing breakfast. It was a cold morning, and they all wore coats. They were drinking something hot from a thermos.

"Hello," said the older man. He had a nice smile.

"Hello," said Jessica. "I guess we're all here for the same thing."

"A new Ryde driver?" asked the young man. Jessica grinned and nodded. The man stood up and shook her hand. "I'm Nur Ali."

The middle-aged woman spoke up. "Would you like some coffee?" She lifted an extra cup.

"Yes!" said Jessica. She left her apartment so early that she didn't have time to make coffee. She sat down with the others at the picnic table. She sipped the warm coffee.

"You saved my life," said Jessica.

"You're welcome," said the woman. "I'm Maria, by the way."

"I'm Hank," said the older man.

"I'm Jessica," said Jessica. "Nice to meet you."

All four of them sat and talked. They got to know each other. As they talked, the sun came up in the east. It was red, then gold. Then they saw two planes arriving. One came from the east. It was the Dallas flight. The other came from the south. That was the Houston flight. It was eight a.m. They all turned on their Ryde apps. Within ten minutes, Hank got a call, and he left. Then Maria left. Then Nur Ali. Then Jessica got a call. Her passenger wanted to go to an office building downtown.

Jessica pulled up to the airport. She saw the passenger, a middle-aged man. She helped him with his suitcase. Then she drove to where he needed to go. He didn't talk much. Mainly he texted and talked on his cell phone. He had a lot of business to do. And he was only in town for one day.

When they got to the office building, the passenger handed her ten dollars. "I have to fly out tonight at seven. Are you working then?"

"Yes," said Jessica.

"Alright. I ask for Jessica, correct?" said the man.

"Yes, that's me," said Jessica. Then she got another call on her Ryde app. There was another passenger at the airport who needed a ride.

CHAPTER NINE

After five days of going to the cell phone lot, Jessica had a bit more money. She made a payment on her Nissan. Then she stopped by to talk to Lucy Pettit and pay the rest of her rent. The apartment manager looked worried, as usual. But she was happy to see the money.

"Are things working out for you?" she asked.

"Yes, ma'am," said Jessica. "I'm working for Ryde Driving Service. This week was a good week."

"Oh yes," said Lucy Pettit. "That's why you're driving the big silver car. I'm used to seeing you in the little red car."

"Right," said Jessica. "The silver car

is my dad's. He's driving my car while I use his."

"He sounds like a good dad," said Lucy. Jessica turned pink and couldn't say anything.

Later that day, Jessica met Lucy's sister. They sat at a table in a coffee shop. The bride, whose name was Penny, was a woman of about twenty-five. She looked a little like Lucy, but she was taller, and she had red hair. Penny was excited about her wedding. She said, "I can't sleep! I'm getting married in just a few days!"

"It will be great," said Jessica. "Now, let's talk about your makeup. With your red hair, it should be fun. I have some ideas. Can you show me your dress? Do you have a close-up picture?"

Penny pulled out her smartphone and showed Jessica a picture of a beautiful, romantic white dress. "Wow," said Jessica. "That will look great with your hair! So, what time is the wedding?"

"Two p.m., day after tomorrow," said Penny. She laughed a little. "I'm not sure I can wait until then!"

Jessica laughed, too. "You'll be fine," she said. "I'll meet you at the church at twelve thirty. That will give me lots of time to do your makeup. And you have four bridesmaids?"

"That's right," said Penny. Then she handed Jessica two hundred dollars. "This is half for now. I can pay the other half after the wedding."

"Fair enough," said Jessica. Now she

had some extra money for rent next month.

It was time to go to the cell phone lot at the airport. The seven p.m. flights from Dallas, Houston, and Oklahoma City would be coming in. When she sat down in the big silver Genesis, Jessica got a text from her father. "Will meet you at the cell phone lot," it said. "I'll have something for you to eat."

Jessica texted back: "Dad! You don't have to do that!"

Juan replied: "Ha!!"

And sure enough, by six p.m., he was at the cell phone lot. It was late February, and the sky was getting dark. A cold, dry wind was blowing. Yet Jessica's three Ryde Driving Service friends were sitting at the picnic table.

Juan Valdez got out of the little red 370Z. He carried a large bag of home-cooked food. Jessica introduced her father.

Juan said, "*Amor*, did you think I could forget your birthday?" Everyone laughed and clapped. And for the next thirty minutes, until the flights came in, everyone enjoyed Juan's good food. They had hot coffee and tortillas with soft chicken and a rich hot sauce.

CHAPTER TEN

Penny's wedding day came. Jessica was at the church at twelve thirty. Penny looked wonderful in her white dress. Her red hair was piled up on her head. Jessica suggested they make a small curl of hair at the back of her neck. Penny loved the idea. Jessica finished her makeup in no time at all. She gave Penny perfect skin and dark eyebrows. Then she finished up with dark pink lipstick and rosy blush. The four bridesmaids came forward so Jessica could do their makeup, too. All four had dark hair. Jessica felt like an artist. She could make women more beautiful. She really missed her job at Wintergreen Drug Store.

Just as she finished, someone came

into the bride's room. This was the room where the bride stayed until the wedding. It was Cammie! Jessica went over to her makeup bag. She wanted to leave without talking to Cammie.

There was a small silence. "Oh, Cammie," said Penny. "Hi."

One or two of the bridesmaids said "Hi" softly. *This is strange*, thought Jessica. *No one seems that happy to see Cammie.*

But Cammie didn't notice that. "I'm so happy to see you!" she said, moving closer to the bride. "But you never asked me to be your bridesmaid!" she said, laughing. "How could you forget?"

"Oh . . . uh," said Penny.

"And who did your makeup? It

looks perfect!" said Cammie. She made the word sound like "*puuuuurrrfect.*"

"Oh, Jessica did that," said one of the bridesmaids. The girl seemed happy to change the topic.

Cammie looked over at Jessica. It was scary how fast her face changed. "What are *you* doing here?" she said. Penny and the bridesmaids gasped.

"Now, wait just a minute," said Penny.

Jessica didn't say anything. She just looked at Cammie. She didn't have to answer Cammie's stupid questions.

"I asked, *what are you doing here?*" said Cammie. Jessica just shook her head. She kept looking at Cammie. Her face was calm.

At just that moment, Lucy came in.

"What's going on in here? I heard loud voices."

"Cammie showed up," said Penny. "Can you get her out of here? She's making trouble. As usual."

Lucy stood in front of Cammie. Cammie looked angry. With her pink lips and blond hair, she looked like a scary doll. "All right, you," said Lucy. "Time to go."

Cammie turned around and pointed at Jessica. "I hope you know you have a thief in here!" Then she left the room.

Lucy sat down and sighed. "That Cammie is trouble. Did you invite her?" she asked Penny.

"No!" said Penny.

"Well, I'll go out and make sure she leaves," said Lucy.

"How do you know her?" said Jessica.

"Oh, she went to high school with me," said Penny. "But I never spent any time with her. She always stole things from drugstores and shops. Makeup. Stuff like that."

CHAPTER ELEVEN

The following morning, Hank was the only other Ryde driver at the cell phone lot. "Nur Ali's wife just had a baby boy," he said. "I don't know where Maria is." He handed Jessica a cup of coffee.

"A baby?" said Jessica. "That's great!"

"Yes," said Hank. "It's their third child. But this is their first boy."

"Wow! Three kids," said Jessica.

"Yeah, he sent me a picture," said Hank. He showed her a photo of a pretty lady. She was smiling. She held a tiny, tiny baby in a blanket.

"Wow, that is so great," said Jessica. And Jessica and Hank drank their coffee. After a few minutes, Jessica asked, "Hank, why do you work for Ryde?"

"Oh," said Hank. "I was an engineer. I worked for Potter Corporation until a few years ago. Then I retired. Then . . . " He stopped talking. Jessica waited.

"Then," he said, "my wife left me."

"What?" said Jessica, surprised. Hank was older, but he was a nice-looking man. He had a warm smile. He dressed well and was a good listener.

"Yes," said Hank. "She fell in love with someone else. Someone at work. I was retired, so I spent a lot of time at home. My wife had a part-time job in an office. I wanted to spend more time together. Maybe take a trip. I looked at vacations to Iceland, Italy, Japan. You name it. But nothing interested her. She said she was too busy at work."

"Huh . . . ," said Jessica.

"Then one week I went to visit my brother in Denver. When I got home, my wife had left all my things at the front door. Two suitcases and a few boxes. She told me, 'Just put the stuff in your car and leave.'"

"*What?*" said Jessica. She couldn't believe it.

"I did no such thing, of course," said Hank. "I got out of my car. I tried to talk to her. She wouldn't even go into the house with me. She told me, 'I've changed the locks. If you need to talk to me, call my lawyer.'" Hank sighed and continued, "I asked her, 'Why are you doing this?' I felt like my life was ending. We had two children together. We were married for thirty years."

"Oh my!" said Jessica. She could not imagine her mother saying such things to her father.

"Well, anyway, I left," said Hank. "I moved into a hotel. I got a lawyer. My lawyer found out she was seeing another man. We're in the middle of a divorce now. I need money. I want to get out and meet people. I don't want to work for my old company. Ryde is perfect for me! I got to meet Nur Ali, and you, and Maria. I like every Ryde driver I meet. It's okay, for now."

"Yes," said Jessica. "It's true. I enjoy my time in the cell phone lot. I can't wait for spring to come, though. I will like this place even better when it warms up a little."

Hank laughed.

Just then, both Hank and Jessica's Ryde apps came up. The flights from Dallas and Houston landed. People wanted rides.

"Thanks for telling me, Hank," said Jessica. "I'm sorry that happened to you."

"Yes," said Hank. "Everyone has a little sadness. That's mine."

CHAPTER TWELVE

In the following week, Jessica did well enough. Between her driving and doing makeup at another wedding, she had enough money to pay all of her rent. She also had enough to make another payment on her Nissan. She liked driving the Genesis, but she missed her fast little car. So far, her father seemed happy with the red car. He seemed happy for Jessica to drive his big car.

Jessica had dinner with Juan two or three times a week now. Her father wanted to teach her how to cook tamales and other delicious food from Mexico. Tonight, they made chile rellenos. These were dark green chiles filled with delicious yellow cheese. You fried the chiles, and the cheese melted inside. They turned out perfectly!

Juan wanted to know if Officer White called.

"No," said Jessica.

"Then it's time for us to visit," said Juan. Jessica agreed to meet her father at the police station at ten a.m. the next day.

Then Jessica said, "I did talk to Mr. Stamps in Dallas."

Juan looked up in surprise. "Oh?" he said.

"Yes," said Jessica. "He said he was still getting information. He also asked if I had found another job yet. I told him I was driving for Ryde. And that I was doing makeup at weddings."

"Oh. What did he say?" asked Juan.

"He said he might have some news for me next week," she said.

"Well, that's something," said Juan.

Nur Ali, Hank, Maria, and Jessica were waiting at the cell phone lot. They shared coffee and breakfast at the picnic table. Jessica asked where Maria was the day before. "Oh, I visited my mother in Albuquerque," said Maria. "I took a few days off. Mom's sick. I want her to move here to be with me. But she doesn't want to."

"Ah," said Hank and Jessica together.

"Anyway, how are you all doing?" said Maria.

"My wife and I had our third child," said Nur Ali.

"That's wonderful!" said Maria. "Are the mother and child both okay?"

"Yes, very well," said Nur Ali. "We wanted her mother and father to come from Jordan to help with our new little boy. But they couldn't make it."

"I'm sorry to hear that," said Hank. "It must be tough to be home with a new baby. And with two other young children!"

"I told my wife, 'I will be your husband, and your mother, and your father!'" said Nur Ali. Everyone laughed.

Jessica thought she would ask her father to make some food for Nur Ali and his wife. They could take it over to their home. That might help a little.

The morning flights came in right on time. Jessica had three different people to drive around. Then she met her father at the police station. They talked to Officer White.

"I talked to the manager at Wintergreen," the officer said. "I told him it was strange that he didn't make a police report. He didn't have a good explanation. But I have some other information that I can't tell you about yet. In a few days, I might have some good news for you."

CHAPTER THIRTEEN

News got around about Jessica's skill with makeup. By the beginning of March, she had three more wedding jobs lined up! She enjoyed driving for Ryde, but she missed her old job at Wintergreen Drug Stores. She loved studying makeup. She wanted to know about all of the new product lines. She missed unpacking shipments from London, or California, or New York. And she loved giving advice and suggestions to people about their skin. It was exciting work.

But for now, she continued her visits to the cell phone lot at the airport. She always had three or four passengers in the morning, and then two or three in the evening. The Ryde passengers seemed endless. Jessica never knew the airport in her town was so busy.

Every day, the cell phone lot regulars spent time talking and sharing coffee and food. Nur Ali thanked Jessica and her father for bringing food over to his home. "We loved it," he said. "Where did your father learn to cook like that? My wife was so happy to take a break from cooking."

"From his mother and grandmother in Mexico," said Jessica. "My mother never cooked. My dad always did."

"It looks like the flight from Dallas is early," said Hank. The plane was like a bright star in the sky. They all watched as the airplane came lower and lower, and then landed. Jessica's Ryde app sent a message. She had a passenger. She gasped when she saw the passenger's name and picture. It was Mr. Stamps! From the Dallas office of Wintergreen Drug Stores! What was he doing in town? Jessica drove up to the airport. Sure enough, there was Mr. Stamps. He got into the back of the Genesis.

"Hello, Ms. Vasquez," he said. He reached forward and shook her hand.

"Mr. Stamps! Where can I take you?" Jessica was so surprised she could hardly talk.

"Let's start with the two Wintergreen Drug Stores near the university. Let me put it in my Ryde app," he said. "Then I have an appointment to visit the police station at two p.m. Oh . . . and I would like to take you for coffee around three p.m. Will you be free?"

"Police station?" asked Jessica. She felt a *thump* in her chest.

"Ah . . ." Mr. Stamps took a piece of paper from his coat pocket and looked at it. "Yes. I want to see someone named Officer White. Do you know him?"

"Yes," said Jessica. She couldn't say anything more. They were silent for the rest of the drive. *What's going on?* she thought. *What's he doing here?*

Jessica felt excited. She dropped Mr. Stamps off at the first Wintergreen on his app. After ten minutes, he came out of the store. Then they drove to the other store. Now Jessica felt bad. This was the store where Cammie and her father worked. In fact, Cammie, her father, and two other employees were waiting for Mr. Stamps at the front of the store. As Mr. Stamps got out of the Genesis, Cammie saw Jessica. And she saw the Ryde Driving Service sign on the car. She said something to her father and pointed. Then she laughed. Her father did not laugh back. Mr. Stamps said to Jessica, "Watch your Ryde app. I may be done early."

"All right Mr. Stamps," said Jessica. She drove away. Then she called her father.

CHAPTER FOURTEEN

Jessica waited at her apartment after lunch. She kept her Ryde app on. She watched it carefully. When she couldn't sit still any longer, she went out to clean the Genesis. Again. Lucy Pettit came out to say hello.

"Penny thought your makeup work was great," she said. "She said that except for Cammie, she loved the wedding."

"I'm glad to hear that," said Jessica. "I love working with makeup and skin care. I want to get back to it."

"Yes, I can see that," said Lucy. She said goodbye and went back into the apartment building's office. While Jessica cleaned the Genesis, she saw a few of her neighbors come out of the apartment building. To her surprise, one of them, a young woman dressed in expensive clothes, had a white envelope in her hands. Jessica knew what it was. It was a "late rent" note. This professional-looking woman was having trouble. Jessica said "Hello" as she walked by. But the young woman didn't answer. Her face didn't change a bit.

That's sad, thought Jessica. *She just wants everything to look like it's perfect.* Jessica wondered whether she would ever make any friends at the apartment building.

Then, at one thirty, Jessica's Ryde app sent a message. Mr. Stamps was ready to go to the police station to see Officer White. Jessica picked him up and then waited for him outside the police station. Just ten minutes later, Mr. Stamps came back out. Officer White was with him! He knocked on her car window and she opened it.

"How are you, Ms. Vasquez?" asked the officer.

"Um," said Jessica. "Fine." Was Officer White smiling? Jessica couldn't tell.

Finally, he said, "Well, I'm sure you and Mr. Stamps have a lot to talk about. See you." And he stood and watched as Jessica drove away. She knew because she saw him in her rearview mirror.

Mr. Stamps asked her to drive to a coffee shop near the college. As they walked into the shop, Jessica's heart went *thumpa-thumpa-thumpa*. They sat down at a table. A waiter brought them each a hot latte.

"Well, Ms. Vasquez," said Mr. Stamps, "I would like you to work for Wintergreen Drug Stores again. As a cosmetics manager."

Jessica was so happy that she couldn't speak. "Really?" was all she could say.

"Yes," said Mr. Stamps. "But now I would like you to work in Albuquerque. We have ten stores there. Very large stores. We are trying some new ideas there with our makeup lines and beauty departments. It would be quite a bit more money for you."

"But why?" asked Jessica.

"Well, Ms. Vasquez," said Mr. Stamps, "after that store manager called us, I got some phone calls from the managers at other stores. They wanted you to come back. Their makeup sales were down. There was no one to help customers. I also got a phone call from the manager at the Wintergreen near the college. Cammie got a part-time job there. She wanted to be their cosmetics manager. The manager didn't want her, but because she knew Cammie's father, she agreed. After just a week, makeup and perfume and shampoo went missing. A lot of it. So she fired Cammie— and she filed a police report. That's why I stopped to talk to Officer White."

"Oh . . . " said Jessica.

"But Cammie was still working at her father's store," said Mr. Stamps. "At least until today. Actually, Cammie's father may lose his job, too. It's against the rules for employees to hire family members to work for them. I think he was hiding Cammie's stealing. Now Cammie may be getting a visit from the police."

Mr. Stamps took a deep breath. "I'm very sorry about all this, Jessica," he said. "I know this was very tough for you. I really want you to think about a fresh start in Albuquerque. You could do great work for us."

"I don't know what to say," said Jessica. Albuquerque was six hours away. But it was a large city. In a beautiful state. She could do well there. It was an exciting idea.

CHAPTER FIFTEEN

In the end, Jessica said yes. She decided to try a new life in Albuquerque. Mr. Stamps wanted her to start in two weeks. That would give her enough time to move out of her apartment and find a new place in Albuquerque. When Jessica told the Ryde drivers at the cell phone lot the next morning, they congratulated her.

Then she told them the story of how she became a Ryde driver. She told them about Cammie and her father. She told them how she lost her job. And how she got the idea to be a Ryde driver. Hank listened carefully. Then he said, "So you have your own little sadness, too."

"Yes," said Jessica. "Everything I dreamed of and worked for was gone. Or I thought so."

Hank nodded. He smiled, but he looked a little sad, too. Jessica thought that maybe his divorce was not yet over. He still had to deal with lawyers. And his awful wife.

There are little sadnesses for all of us, Jessica thought. *Little things that set us back. Small, unkind people who set us back. Like Cammie and Hank's wife.*

Maria called her mother in Albuquerque while they waited for the morning flights to come in. Maria then told Jessica that if she needed a place to stay, she was welcome to stay with her mother.

"It's a huge old house," she said to

Jessica. "Even if you just stay a few days, it will make her very happy."

Jessica gave her last rides with Ryde that morning. Then she turned off her Ryde app and got ready to leave the town she grew up in.

To Jessica's surprise, her father was totally happy about the move. "*Amor*, this is wonderful news!" he said. They were having dinner at Jessica's apartment. It was full of boxes. She was already packing her things. "You know, these chile rellenos you made are good," Juan said. Jessica laughed. But then he said something that surprised her even more. "I've been thinking about giving up the house-painting business," he said. "I'm ready to do something new. I have lots of money. Your brother and sister are doing well. Your mother's gone. I don't have anything left here."

"What would you like to do?" asked Jessica. But she had an idea.

"If you like, I will help you move to Albuquerque," said her father.

"Yes, I'd like that, Dad," said Jessica. "And why don't you stay for a while?"

"I'd like that too, *amor*," said Juan. "I want you to show me how to use the Ryde app. With the Genesis, I can give rides to passengers in Albuquerque. Why not? At least until I decide what I want to do."

Jessica felt a deep happiness. But that night, she got a call from her sister in college. "What are you doing?"

said Veronica. "Why did you give Dad this stupid idea about moving to Albuquerque?"

"It wasn't my idea," said Jessica. "It was Dad's idea. And it's not stupid. Now just stop it. Grow up! And after you decide to do that, come visit us in Albuquerque."

It wasn't a happy phone call. But Jessica felt good. Her life wasn't over. It was just beginning again, in a new way. It would be spring soon. There would be brighter days.